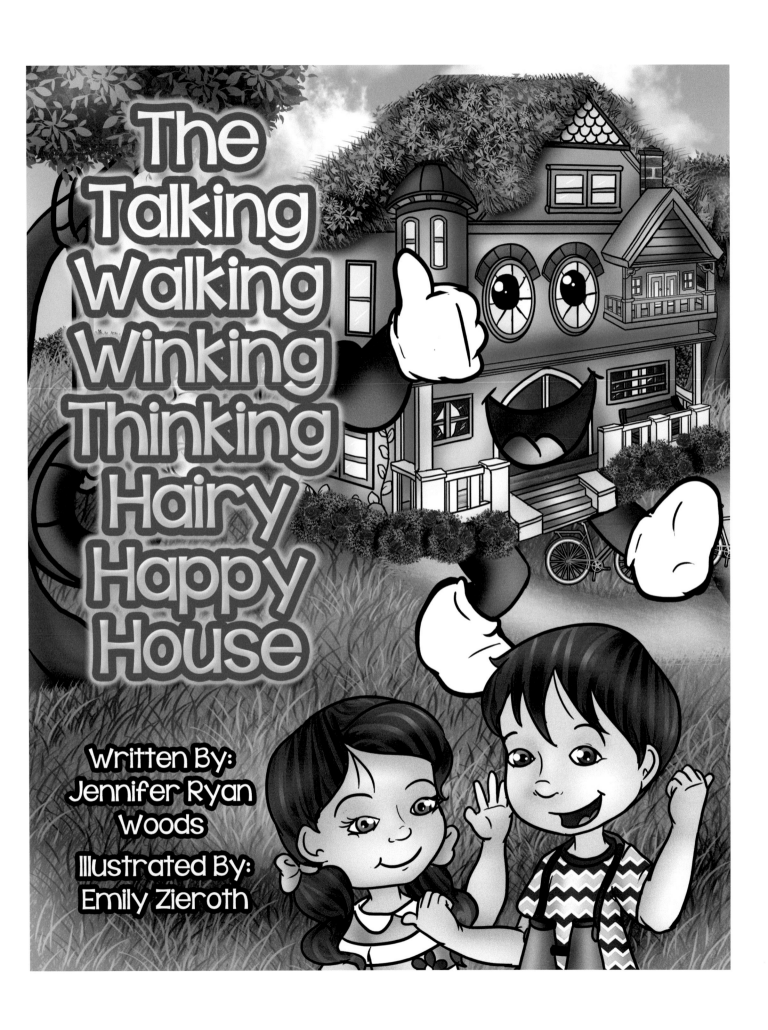

The Talking Walking Winking Thinking Hairy Happy House

Written By:
Jennifer Ryan Woods

Illustrated By:
Emily Zieroth

To order additional copies of this book, contact:
Xlibris
1-888-795-4274
www.Xlibris.com
Orders@Xlibris.com

To my spectacular daughters, Ella and Audrey: You were the sole inspiration for this book and you continue to inspire me everyday in everything that I do.

To my husband Michael: Thank you for doing everything in your power to help make my dreams come true.

Thank you to my family and friends who read countless drafts of this book! Your input was vital in bringing it to life.

I'm Jack, this is Jenny. We're sister and brother.
We live in this house with our father and mother.

It may look like any old house on the block,
So when you hear the truth, it may come as a SHOCK!!

4

Our two little doggies, Meatball and
Spaghetti --
are the only ones that we've told already.

Now we'll share it with you, on the count of
five...
Our house...where we live...it's actually
ALIVE!

Now before you say that cannot be true,
Give us a minute. We'll prove it to you!

It started last week, out in our front yard.
Something peculiar caught me off guard.

6

On the front of my house, I noticed a pair...
of windows that made me look up and stare.

I looked at those windows from there on the
ground.
They looked really funny, so BIG and so
round.

When I realized why, I gasped in surprised!
Those windows, I thought, looked like a pair
of EYES!

Pupils *in* the middle! Eyelashes on top!
The sight made me laugh and I just couldn't stop!

Then Jenny called to me, "What's so funny Jack?"
When I showed her, she had a giggle attack.

She laughed so hard she fell into Mom's *plants*.
I thought she was going to *pee in her pants*!

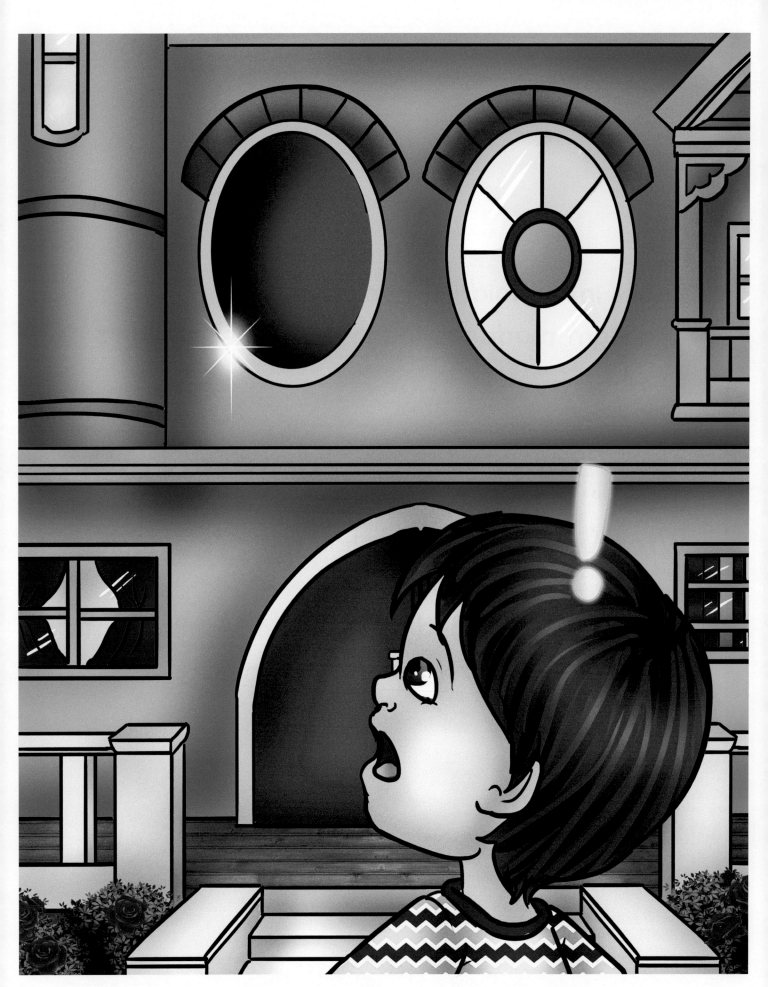

But then something happened that you'd never think.
A window looked at me, then gave me a wink!

I glanced at that window a moment and then...
It glanced back at me and it winked AGAIN!

The shock made me fall into a rose bush.
I yelled "OUCH!" as a thorn poked me in my tush.

Then Mommy came running. "Jack are you OK?"
I just nodded my head. What else could I say?

Later that night as I snuggled in bed,
I could not get that window out of my head.

I HAD to tell Jenny about that wink.
But would she believe me? What would she think?

I told her at last and when I was through, she just smiled and said "well, what should we do?"

We decided that we would investigate.
We were so excited. We could barely wait!

The next morning after we saw the sun rise,
We jumped out of *bed* and gathered supplies.

We ran out of the house and down the driveway.
There was work to do. This was no time to play!

We stared at the house and took in the view.
And then Jenny spotted it! CLUE #2!

She pointed up toward the top of the roof.
She said, "Look Jack! I found even more proof."

From down below we could see it up there.
We saw that the roof was covered with HAIR!

It was piled up high in a messy hairdo.
It looked like it needed a lot of shampoo!

Then something made me look down at the door.
Could that be ANOTHER clue to explore?

I thought: maybe the door is part of a face.
If it were a mouth, it'd be in the right place.

We focused our eyes on the door for awhile.
Then all of the sudden, it started to SMILE!

Now I was sure, this was a mouth INDEED.
Jenny said that she completely agreed.

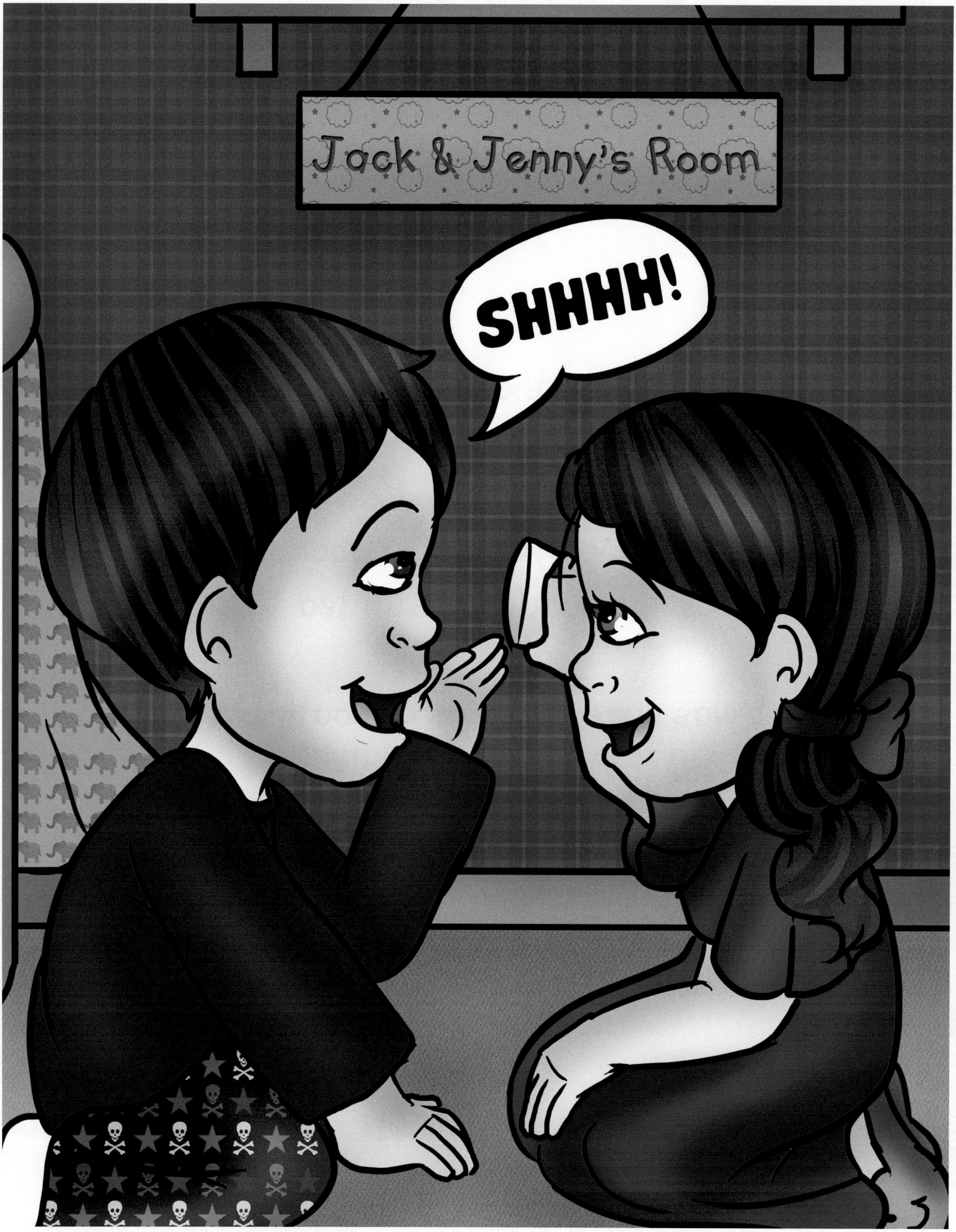
Jack & Jenny's Room
SHHHH!

Suddenly a new thought popped into my mind,
There was one more clue that I needed to find.

That night in our room when I turned off the light
We whispered softly to the house "Goodnight."

A few moments later we heard a soft creak.
Then it grew louder. Did our house just speak?

Jenny thought maybe it came from the floor,
Or perhaps a pipe or an old squeaky door.

We listened real hard, our ears pressed to the wall.
We heard a new sound. It started out small.

As it grew louder we heard what it said!
"Goodnight Jenny and Jack. It's time for bed."

Now we know our house talks. It can see. It can hear.
But some other things are a little unclear.

We're not sure if it can get up and move,
and this is something that's *been* tricky to prove.

Our house will not tell us, not Jenny or me,
but you *probably* guessed...I have a theory!

I think that at night around 10 o'clock,
Our house takes a little stroll down the block.

I bet it has house friends that live on the street,
And when we're asleep, they get up and meet!

28

We may never find out, but that's no big deal.
We're happy enough knowing our house is real!!

You may not believe us, but I hope you do, because if you believe, you may see it too!

Printed in the United States
By Bookmasters